# River Otter at Autumn Lane

Book copyright © 2002 Trudy Corporation and the Smithsonian Institution, Washington DC 20560.

Published by Soundprints Division of Trudy Corporation, Norwalk, Connecticut.

Book layout: Marcin D. Pilchowski
Editor: Ashley C. Andersen
Editorial assistance: Chelsea Shriver

First Edition 2002
10 9 8 7 6 5 4 3 2 1
Printed in Singapore

*Acknowledgments:*
   Our very special thanks to Dr. Don E. Wilson of the Department of Systematic Biology at the Smithsonian Institution's National Museum of Natural History for his curatorial review.
   Soundprints would also like to thank Ellen Nanney and Robyn Bissette at the Smithsonian Institution's Office of Product Development and Licensing for their help in the creation of this book.

*Library of Congress Cataloging-in-Publication Data is on file with the publisher and the Library of Congress.*

# River Otter at Autumn Lane

by Laura Gates Galvin
Illustrated by Christopher Leeper

**Soundprints**
Where Children Discover...

After a long, snowy winter in Vermont, spring has finally arrived. Behind an old white farmhouse on Autumn Lane, runs a lazy stretch of river. At the river's edge, in a den between the roots of fallen trees, a river otter is nursing her three newborn cubs.

River Otter's cubs are tiny, blind and helpless. After only a few moments of suckling, they fall fast asleep.

Before the cubs were born, River Otter worked hard to make a cozy nest for them. She carried bunches of dried leaves in her mouth, bringing them through a tangle of tree roots hiding the entrance to a tunnel. The tunnel once led to a beaver's den. Now River Otter has made the empty den her home.

River Otter is hungry. She leaves her sleeping cubs to find food. Another tunnel at the other end of the den leads her directly into the river. On her belly, River Otter slides smoothly through the tunnel and into the water. She dives straight to the bottom to look for her favorite meal—crayfish.

River Otter pokes her nose into cracks
and under rocks. Her stiff whiskers feel around for
food. Under a large rock, her whiskers detect a movement.
It is a crayfish. River Otter digs under the rock with her nose
and grabs the crayfish in her mouth. She carries her tasty meal
to the water's surface and eats it.

By early July, the days are warm and long. Fields of tall grass feed the flocks of sheep and the cows by the old white farmhouse. River Otter's cubs have spent the last three months in their den, eating, sleeping—and growing! They are almost twice as big as they were at birth and they can now see and hear.

River Otter plays with her cubs often. She rolls around in a ball with them. She gives them rides on her back. When River Otter takes short trips to get food, the cubs continue to play in the den, wrestling and tumbling with each other.

The cubs have not left the den yet, but River Otter knows the time has come for them to explore their world. She leads them out of the den to the river's edge. The cubs stagger behind her. Their legs are still a bit weak and wobbly. They tumble and trip, and finally gain their balance.

River Otter slides down a muddy slope and lands with a splash in the river. She swims a short distance and then chirps and squeaks, calling her babies into the water. The cubs look on, terrified. They do not want to go into the cool, dark river.

River Otter chirps and squeaks again. Still, the cubs don't budge. River Otter swims to the surface and climbs up the riverbank. With her nose, she nudges each cub toward the water. The cubs simply cannot be coaxed into a swimming lesson!

Finally, River Otter has no choice but to pick up the cubs by the scruffs of their necks and drag them to the water, plopping them in one by one. At first, the cubs just bob up and down. One cub tries to scramble up the riverbank, but River Otter drags him right back into the water.

After a few days, River Otter's cubs are at home in the river. They watch their mother as she dives for crayfish and mud minnows. They watch her catch eels and frogs. The cubs don't catch their own food right away—River Otter brings food to the shore for them to eat. But very soon, River Otter will teach them how to dive and catch food for themselves.

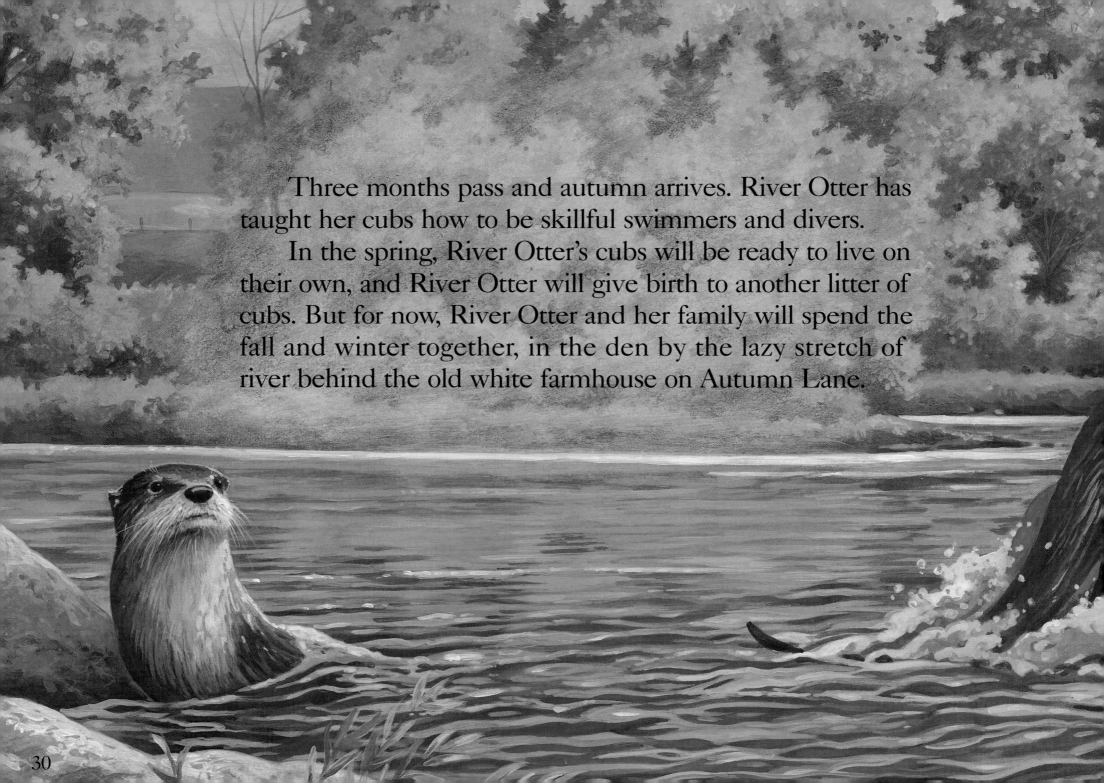

Three months pass and autumn arrives. River Otter has taught her cubs how to be skillful swimmers and divers.

In the spring, River Otter's cubs will be ready to live on their own, and River Otter will give birth to another litter of cubs. But for now, River Otter and her family will spend the fall and winter together, in the den by the lazy stretch of river behind the old white farmhouse on Autumn Lane.

## About the River Otter

River otters belong to the family *Mustelidae*, which includes weasels, badgers and skunks. River otters live on all continents except Australia and Antarctica. They live along streambeds, rivers and marshes and spend a great amount of time in the water. They can stay under water for three to four minutes before coming up for air. River otters have special muscles that allow them to close their ears and nostrils tightly to keep water out.

Most river otters weigh from 10 to 30 pounds, and grow between 3 and 4 feet long, including their tails. Their fur varies in color from brownish-gray to dark brown when dry, and darker when wet. River otters have small flat heads, long thick necks and thick tails that narrow to a point.

River otters eat crayfish, crabs and fish. Sometimes they can catch fast-swimming fish like trout, but usually they capture slower fish. They also eat frogs, insects and snakes.

Most river otters live in the abandoned dens of other animals, or under rocky ledges. Female river otters give birth to two or three cubs or pups at a time.

## Glossary

*crayfish:* A freshwater crustacean that looks like a small lobster.
*cubs:* The name used for baby river otters, also called pups.
*den:* A sheltered home a river otter lives in after another animal moves out of it.
*mud minnows:* Small fish found in the mud.

*webbed feet:* Feet with toes that are connected by tissue, similar to ducks' feet.

## Points of Interest in This Book

*pp. 4-5:* American robin; Canada geese.
*pp. 10-11:* crayfish.
*pp. 14-15:* trout lily (yellow flowers)

*pp. 22-23:* dragonfly.
*pp. 28-29:* mud minnow (bottom left); frog (upper right)
*pp. 30-31:* water willow (bottom left).